What Kids Say About
Carole Marsh Mysteries . . .

I love the real locations! Reading the book always makes me want to go and visit them all on our next family vacation. My Mom says maybe, but I can't wait!

One day, I want to be a real kid in one of Ms. Marsh's mystery books. I think it would be fun, and I think I am a real character anyway. I filled out the application and sent it in and am keeping my fingers crossed!

History was not my favorite subject till I starting reading Carole Marsh Mysteries. Ms. Marsh really brings history to life. Also, she leaves room for the scary and fun.

I think Christina is so smart and brave. She is lucky to be in the mystery books because she gets to go to a lot of places. I always wonder just how much of the book is true and what is made up. Trying to figure that out is fun!

Grant is cool and funny! He makes me laugh a lot!!

I like that there are boys and girls in the story of different ages. Some mysteries I outgrow, but I can always find a favorite character to identify with in these books.

They are scary, but not too scary. They are funny. I learn a lot. There is always food which makes me hungry. I feel like I am there.

What Parents and Teachers Say About Carole Marsh Mysteries . . .

I think kids love these books because they have such a wealth of detail. I know I learn a lot reading them! It's an engaging way to look at the history of any place or event. I always say I'm only going to read one chapter to the kids, but that never happens—it's always two or three, at least!
—Librarian

Reading the mystery and going on the field trip—Scavenger Hunt in hand—was the most fun our class ever had! It really brought the place and its history to life. They loved the real kids characters and all the humor. I loved seeing them learn that reading is an experience to enjoy!
—4th grade teacher

Carole Marsh is really on to something with these unique mysteries. They are so clever; kids want to read them all. The Teacher's Guides are chock full of activities, recipes, and additional fascinating information. My kids thought I was an expert on the subject—and with this tool, I felt like it!
—3rd grade teacher

My students loved writing their own Real Kids/Real Places mystery book! Ms. Marsh's reproducible guidelines are a real jewel. They learned about copyright and more & ended up with their own book they were so proud of!
—Reading/Writing Teacher

"The kids seem very realistic—my children seemed to relate to the characters. Also, it is educational by expanding their knowledge about the famous places in the books."

"They are what children like: mysteries and adventures with children they can relate to."

"Encourages reading for pleasure."

"This series is great. It can be used for reluctant readers, and as a history supplement."

The Awesome Aquarium Mystery!

by Carole Marsh

Published by Gallopade International/Carole Marsh Books. Printed in the
United States of America.

Managing Editor: Sherry Moss
Cover Design: Michele Winkelman
Picture Credits:
The publisher would like to thank the following for their kind permission to
reproduce the cover images.
©2006 JupiterImages Corporation *Lion Fish;*
J.P. Kollhøj, Norway *Clown Fish;*
Jeff Williams *Sea Turtle*

Gallopade is proud to be a member and supporter of these educational
organizations and associations:

American Booksellers Association
International Reading Association
National Association for Gifted Children
The National School Supply and Equipment Association
The National Council for the Social Studies
Museum Store Association
Association of Partners for Public Lands

This book is a complete work of fiction. All events are fictionalized, and
although the names of real people are used, their characterization in this
book is fiction. The words attributed to Mr. Marcus are purely fictional.

Jell-O® is a registered trademark of Kraft Foods.

20 Years Ago . . .

As a mother and an author, one of the fondest periods of my life was when I decided to write mystery books for children. At this time (1979) kids were pretty much glued to the TV, something parents and teachers complained about the way they do about web surfing and blogging today.

I decided to set each mystery in a real place—a place kids could go and visit for themselves after reading the book. And I also used real children as characters. Usually a couple of my own children served as characters, and I had no trouble recruiting kids from the book's location to also be characters.

Also, I wanted all the kids—boys and girls of all ages—to participate in solving the mystery. And, I wanted kids to learn something as they read. Something about the history of the location. And I wanted the stories to be funny. That formula of real+scary+smart+fun served me well.

I love getting letters from teachers and parents who say they read the book with their class or child, then visited the historic site and saw all the places in the mystery for themselves. What's so great about that? What's great is that you and your children have an experience that bonds you together forever. Something you shared. Something you both cared about at the time. Something that crossed all age levels—a good story, a good scare, a good laugh!

20 years later,

Carole Marsh

About the Characters

Christina, age 10: Mysterious things really do happen to her! Hobbies: soccer, Girl Scouts, anything crafty, hanging out with Mimi, and going on new adventures.

Grant, age 7: Always manages to fall off boats, back into cactuses, and find strange clues—even in real life! Hobbies: camping, baseball, computer games, math, and hanging out with Papa.

Mimi is Carole Marsh, children's book author and creator of Carole Marsh Mysteries, Around the World in 80 Mysteries, Awesome Mysteries, Sportsmysteries, and many others.

Papa is Bob Longmeyer, the author's real-life husband, who really does wear a tuxedo, cowboy boots and hat, fly an airplane, captain a boat, speak in a booming voice, and laugh a lot!

Other Titles

Table of Contents

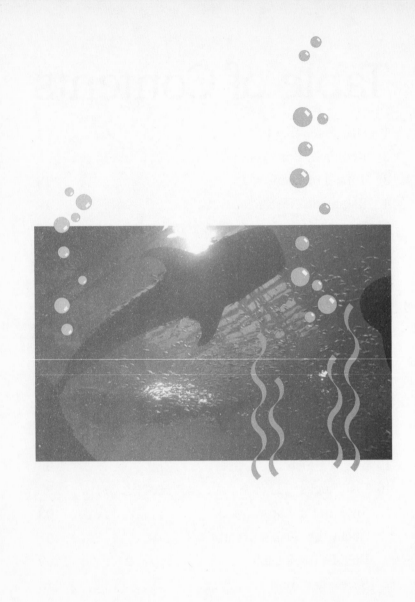

One Fish, Two Fish

It was nine a.m. on the dot. Christina, Grant, Mimi, and Papa had timed ticket reservations to the grand opening of the new aquarium. "And, boy are we excited!" Grant kept repeating over and over and over to anyone who was listening...or not!

"I know you are excited, Grant," said his sister, Christina, age 10, "but can you think of just one other thing to say...please."

Grant stood on one foot and then the other, waiting exceedingly impatiently for the doors to open and allow them into the brand-spanking new aquarium. It was a little damp and chilly, but that was not what was bothering Grant. First and foremost, he really was just plain too excited to stand still...and secondly, he really, really had to go to the bathroom.

"Those fish have it made," Grant finally said.

"What does that mean?" his sister asked, perplexed.

"You don't want to know," Grant said, squirming more and more.

Papa reached down and patted both his grandchildren on their fleece-capped heads. "Just be patient a little longer," he pleaded. He understood that excited seven-year-olds didn't have much patience. "The doors will open any minute; I promise. After all, I need a cup of coffee."

"Don't talk about anything liquid, please," pleaded Grant.

"It's an aquarium, Grant," said his sister. "It's all about liquid."

"Patience, patience," Papa said. "The doors will open any minute."

And as if he had cast a magic spell, the doors to the new aquarium did open. The lucky ticketholders waiting out in the drizzling rain cheered.

"We're pretty near the front of the line," said

Mimi. "It won't take us too long to get inside." Their grandmother swiped at her hair, which was getting curlier by the minute. "I hope!" she added. "Or I will look just like Little Orphan Annie, and what will the fish think of that?"

Grant and Christina giggled. Their grandmother Mimi was a famous children's mystery book writer. Papa was her Big Helper. She had promised that she was just visiting the new aquarium, and had no plans to write a new mystery book. But Grant and Christina knew better.

They had traveled all around the world with Mimi and Papa. Sometimes on airplanes (including Papa's little red and white *Mystery Girl*)...sometimes on trains...or by car...or even rickshaw—and no matter what Mimi said, she *always* wrote a mystery book about their adventures.

Papa held a colorful umbrella he had bought in Paris down lower over Mimi's head as they slowly snaked forward in the line. "So you're not going to write a mystery?" he asked Mimi with a smile. "That sounds very fishy to me."

"VERY fishy!" Christina and Grant agreed.

"Well, what would I write about?" asked

Mimi, grumpily. She was tired and cold and missing her coffee.

Just then, they came to the head of the line. Papa handed the smiling ticket-taker their tickets and they walked inside. As soon as they got inside the door, they all stopped dead in their tracks and looked up, down, and all around.

"Whoa," said Grant. "Maybe you could write about THIS!"

THIS was the newest aquarium to open in America. It was a whopper! In fact, it was proclaimed to be the world's largest aquarium. It was beautiful—especially the dramatic welcoming atrium. They all gasped as they walked past tanks of fish called blue runners. The decorated entrances to the various galleries beckoned invitingly. An interactive wall exhibit let you identify fish by touching a screen as they swam by.

It was clear that the entire place was filled with the latest aquarium technology. It was filled with enormous tanks of water. And it was chockfull of absolutely awesome and fascinating fish. They truly did not know where to begin.

So, needless to say, each of them pointed in a different direction and cried, "Let's go this way!"

Papa laughed. "Where do you want to go, Christina?"

"Let's visit the biggest tank of all, first," she begged. She pointed in one direction where many people were heading toward a gallery called Ocean Voyager.

"How about you?" Papa asked Grant.

Grant squirmed his legs together and pointed to a small door off to the side. "How about there first?" he suggested urgently. Grant pointed to the bathroom.

Mimi nodded and Grant ran off.

"Great!" said Christina. "We wait two years to come to the most famous and humongous aquarium of all time, and I have to spend the first ten minutes waiting for..."

Before she could finish her sentence, her brother reappeared.

"Wow!" his sister said. "That must be an all time record."

"I was in a hurry," her brother said. "I don't want to miss anything."

"Those fish aren't going anywhere," Papa said. "Let's take our time and enjoy our first visit. There's so much to see, I doubt we can see it all in one day anyway." He began to twist and turn to look all around. "Where is she?" he muttered. Mimi had already disappeared. She was more fourth-grader than grandmother and they all knew they would have a hard time keeping up with her.

Christina and Grant giggled.

"Mimi's gone walkabout, I think," said Christina.

Papa sighed. "Well, let's try to catch up," he said. Follow me, and let's don't get lost from one another for a change. Ok? Ok?? OK???" He turned around to find that he was standing all alone. "Oh, brother," he said to no one in particular. "Let the mystery adventure begin!"

Red Fish, Blue Fish

No one knew where Mimi had gone. Grant sped off to the touch tanks. He really liked to get up-close-and-personal with sea life. Papa headed for the cafeteria to grab a cup of hot coffee. Christina walked to the center of the atrium and froze in her tracks.

As people buzzed around her, headed in different directions, and chatting with excitement, Christina just stood there in awe. All around her, as well as above and below, were sights and sounds that intrigued her.

Christina loved lights, and sounds, and colors, and action—and the new aquarium's gigantic entrance hall engaged all her senses. She could hardly take her eyes off an overhead wavy screen showing enormous sea life go by. Entranceways to various parts of the aquarium had special display signs. Each one was bright and entertaining and made her want to rush to all of them at the same time.

The room seemed to be filled with blue and light and the musical sound of the sea. It's just like a dream, she thought to herself. It's beautiful! And I haven't even seen the fish yet, she marveled. She decided that she must look lost because a nice man with an official aquarium tag on his shirt tapped her on the shoulder, and when she spun around, he asked, "Are you lost?"

Christina blushed and giggled. "I don't think so, thank you," she said. "I just got here, and I...I..." She realized that she was speechless and could not explain herself.

Now the man laughed heartily. "I know just how you feel, young lady," he admitted. He waved his arms in an arc over his head to indicate the entire aquarium. "I've been watching this place come to life for more than two years, and I'm still astounded every time I step inside."

Christina looked puzzled. "You've been here

for two years?" she said. "I thought the aquarium just opened today."

"Sorry to confuse you," the man said. He stood up very tall. "I guess you could say that I was sort of the reason...or in charge of...or, well, I've been around since this aquarium was just a little minnow of an idea."

Christina was very impressed. "Then I guess this must be a really big day for you," she said.

"Oh, yes," said the man. "It's like Christmas and my birthday, and loads of other holidays all in one—only better!" He laughed again. "I could take you on a little tour," he offered. "Where is the rest of your family?"

Christina looked around and sighed. "Oh, we got separated right away," she said. "But I would be thrilled if you could point me in the right direction—like maybe to your very favorite part of the aquarium."

The man smiled. "Then let's sit right here," he said, indicating a bench nearby.

They sat down and the man began to tell Christina about the different parts of the aquarium. He talked very fast and with excitement and enthusiasm.

"Now if you want to learn about the coast, you

can head that way," he said, waving an arm at a large lighthouse. "And if you like river creatures, that area will show you some amazing things!" He pointed to an entrance that looked like it led into a special effects movie set for a jungle or rainforest.

Christina nodded and the man continued. "Where you see the snow on the rocks, you can go and see some incredible cold water sea life. And over there is a great barrier reef that's absolutely gorgeous!"

By now, Christina was getting both excited and confused. Then the man surprised her by whispering almost reverently: "See that entrance?" He pointed a finger at a dark area across the hall from where they sat.

Christina nodded again, eager to hear what the man had to say. "Well, that," he said proudly, "is the doorway to the most amazing thing you'll see in this aquarium!" He leaned down and whispered in her ear. "You don't want to miss it...but I won't spoil the surprise by telling you any more. And of course you have to see the really cool 3-D movie and get a delicious snack in the cafeteria, and..."

Before he could continue, an aquarium staff

person ran up to the man. "Excuse me, sir," he said urgently. "Uh, I'm afraid..." he looked at Christina, then lowered his voice. "I'm afraid we have a situation." He said the word more like SITUATION, as if to emphasize that he needed help right away.

The nice man patted Christina on her head like she was a little kid. "Gotta go," he said. "Have fun and perhaps I'll see you later and can hear your impressions of your great new aquarium."

Christina looked puzzled. "My aquarium?" she asked, confused.

"It's a gift," the man said with a big smile. "Enjoy it!" And then he hurried off with the other man.

With a sigh, Christina sat there a moment longer, wondering which way to go and where to start. Usually when faced with such a decision, she did eeny, meenie, miney, mo...or one potato, two potato...but this time she said aloud, as she pointed to each entrance... "One fish, two fish, red fish, blue fish. Ok! Looks like I'm headed for that special door over there."

She shivered with excitement, jumped up and headed across the busy hall, dodging baby strollers, little kids, big parents, and aquarium volunteers. As she peered across the hall to find her way, she noticed that the nice man and the aquarium staffer had just rushed into that very entrance—the sign said Ocean Voyager: Journey with Giants.

A SITUATION, she thought. I wonder what that's all about? My aquarium, she thought. I wonder what he meant? And I wonder where Papa, and Mimi, and Grant are? And I wonder...

But all of a sudden, Christina forgot to wonder because she was suddenly filled with wonder as she entered a...tunnel of water!

Tunnel of Water

"Wooooow!" Christina said as she stared overhead. Above her, fish great and small, seemed to sail through a sky of water.

"Boy, howdy, wow!" said a deep voice behind her. Christina would know that voice anywhere—it was Papa.

"Whoopie, kai-yai WOW!" screeched a young voice. Christina giggled. That could only be Grant.

"Wooooooooooow!" drawled a soft Southern voice. Mimi put her hands on Christina's shoulders. "What do you think of this?" she asked.

"I think I wonder if we have family ESP* to all wind up at the same place at the same time," said Christina. "And I think this is almost like

*Extra Sensory Perception

being in the water with the fishes. It's so cool!"

"COOL!" repeated Grant, who had his nose pressed to the wall of glass as a large grouper surrounded by a cloud of small gold fish silently swam by.

Everyone in the tunnel seemed enthralled with this unique view of the fish. A school of manta rays sailed overhead. Then suddenly, two large shadows appeared out of nowhere. In spite of herself, Christina ducked. The two monstrous fish swam overhead and vanished off into the murky water. Another cloud of the little gold fish whisked past them.

"What was that?!" said Grant. "Giant sharks?"

Mimi shuttered. "I hope not," she said. Mimi did not like things with lots of arms or legs or teeth.

"I don't think they were sharks," said Papa.

"Well, what were they?" Christina asked. She thought Papa knew, but was not telling. He always wanted his grandkids to figure out things on their own. He said that's how you learned to research and to do critical thinking, as he called it.

Papa nudged the others forward through the tunnel. "I think if we keep going, we just might find out," he said.

As much as she hated to leave, Christina led them out of the tunnel and into a dark passageway. "Why is it so dark?" she asked. "It makes it sort of spooky...like a haunted aquarium."

"It's kept dark for the fish," Mimi explained. "Plus I think it actually helps us see them better."

"It's all about the fish, right?" Grant asked.

"It's an aquarium!" Christina reminded her brother.

"It's all about the fish to me," said Papa.

Christina giggled. "But you always say that, Papa. Especially when we go out to eat seafood."

Papa put his finger to his lips. "SHHHHH!" he hissed, pointing at the fish in the next tank window. "I don't want them to think I'm the enemy."

The kids giggled and stood on tiptoes to admire the fish. Christina was torn between reading all the information about the unique and often colorful fish, and moving on to the next tank she was so eager to see.

Slowly, they moved from tank to tank, enjoying the fish...and enjoying seeing little kids *ooh* and *aah* over the fish. Perhaps that's why Christina was not expecting what happened next. She still was at the front of their group when she turned a sharp corner in the darkened passage. And suddenly she came face-to-face with what looked like the entire sea!

Christina stared up at the most gigantic window of glass that she had ever seen. It looked as big as a football field to her. "This must be the biggest fish tank ever!" she said.

An aquarium staffer nearby laughed. "Almost," he said. "This is the second largest aquarium tank window in the world. It's 28 feet tall and 63 feet wide. That's 8.5 meters and 19.2 meters, if you're into metrics," he added.

Grant groaned. "Oh, I'm into metrics," he said. "It's on my next test...the one I haven't studied for."

"What a view!" Mimi cried. "It's like looking right out to sea...or rather I mean it's like looking right out INTO the sea."

"And what do you see in our sea?" the aquarium staffer asked.

Obviously, there were lots of fish in the six million gallon tank. Christina looked around at the hammerhead sharks, sawfish, groupers, and skates. Schools of golden trevally swept by. An unusual bowmouth guitarfish swooped right in front of them.

But suddenly Christina knew why he had asked them that question at that specific moment. For, magically, out of the far reaches of the water appeared a dark shadow that soon turned into an enormous fish. It looked as big as a school bus! And before they all could gasp in glee, another dark polka-dotted shadow, surrounded by a host of the bright gold fish, came forward into full majestic view.

"What are they?" Grant asked in awe.

The staffer stood taller and announced proudly: "They are Ralph and Norton!"

Ralph and Norton

Mimi laughed. "Do you name all your fish?" she asked.

The staffer laughed too. "Well, not all 100,000 of them," he said. "But these two guys are special. They are the largest fish in the world."

"You're kidding, right?" Grant asked, straining his neck to look up at the two humongous creatures. "They're really whales, right? And whales are mammals, not fish. I learned that in Adventure Scouts."

"Ralph and Norton are whale sharks," the staffer explained.

"Ohhh," said Christina, with a shiver. "So

they are giant sharks?"

"No," said the staffer, patiently. It seemed that he had made this explanation quite a few times already today. "They are indeed fish. They are fish called whale sharks. And, like I said, they're the largest species of fish on earth."

"Whale sharks...cool name," said Grant. "They are so big that I guess they're also great-, great-, great-granddaddy fish?"

"Nope," said the staffer. "They are just growing boy fish. When they are full grown, they will be twice as big—about thirty feet long."

"So they'll outgrow this tank?" asked Mimi.

"Oh, no," said the staffer. "There is plenty of room for Ralph and Norton here, now and in the future."

"And how did they get those funky names?" Christina asked.

The staffer laughed. "I'll bet your grandfather knows?" he suggested.

Papa looked pleased. "Oh, yes, I know why they are called Ralph and Norton!" he said.

Christina and Grant looked at one another in surprise. How could Papa know that, they wondered. Today was the first day the aquarium was open. Then Christina figured out it must be something only old people would know. But she would never call Papa old. After all, he dressed like a cowboy—even today at the aquarium—and flew a little red and white airplane called *The Mystery Girl*, and laughed a lot. Plus, he and Mimi went dancing all the time, and Mimi, who was younger than Papa, always wore the latest, most sparkly, and (Papa always said), "the skimpiest" fashions.

"Well I know what I would have named them," said Grant.

"What?" asked the staffer.

"BIG and BIGGER!" said Grant and they all laughed.

As they all continued to stare at the amazing whale sharks, another aquarium staff person came up and tugged on the shirt of the staffer who had been talking to them. "Hey, Joe," he said. "I need you to come with me right now, buddy. We have a real situation."

Christina noted that he said it like SITUATION, too. Hmm, she wondered...what was going on? But she was too enthralled with Ralph and Norton to think about it. If there was a mystery brewing in the aquarium, well, she just didn't have time for it. There was way too much to see. But how, she wondered, was she ever going to drag Grant away from this enormous tank...and who was going to clean up all the fingerprints and nose prints that all the curious kids were leaving all over the glass?

Just then a movie started on one of the high tech screens mounted overhead. Without speaking, they all sat down on the carpeted steps in front of the aquarium to watch. The movie showed how Ralph and Norton had been brought to the aquarium...how the whale sharks were each fed with their own colored scoops—yellow and green...and what they ate, which was a LOT of krill.

"Krill?" said Grant. "Like road krill?"

Papa laughed. "Not road kill," he said, "krill— that's like small shrimp."

"I figured fish this big would eat something like...uh, maybe little kids?"

"Just krill," said Papa. Then the movie showed aquarium workers dumping krill in front of the mouths of the fish and them inhaling it like a vacuum cleaner.

"They eat just like you, Grant," Christina teased her brother.

Grant responded by opening his mouth as

wide as he could and pretending that he was inhaling tons of food.

Mimi, who was absorbed with the whale sharks, had not been paying a lot of attention. When she spotted Grant gulping air like a fish out of water, she waved her hands in submission. "Ok, ok," she said. "If you're that hungry, we'll head to the cafeteria right now!" She herded them away from the giant aquarium window, saying, "We can always come back later."

Little could Mimi have known that before the afternoon was over, she would indeed be staring back inside the tank window...only it would not just be whale sharks she would see. And what she would see would make her...*scream!*

It is the Dawning of the Age of Aquaria

Reluctantly, Christina and Grant followed their grandmother out of the Ocean Voyager exhibit. Papa "rode herd" like a true trail boss behind them. Snaking in and out of the lines and groups and schools and pods of visitors, they finally made their way across the atrium to the Aquaria Food Court.

"Wow," said Christina, "this is the coolest food court I ever saw!" She stared at the array of open-kitchen style windows where chefs were cooking pizza, grilling hamburgers, slapping together mouth-watering sandwiches, or scooping up dishes of ice cream.

"I can see we have some serious choices to make here," said Papa. He dug into his jeans pocket and pulled out bills and divided them among Mimi, Grant, and Christina. "I figure the odds of us all wanting something from the same area is most remote," he said. "So get your food and let's meet right here—he plopped his Stetson hat down on a nearby table.

"I love the décor," Mimi swooned. "Don't you, Christina?"

Christina looked all around. "Oh, yes!" she said. "I love all these orange and aqua colors. They make me think of the beach." Christina loved modern things and the beach, and as she headed for the pizza station, her imagination went wild thinking of how she could redesign her dollhouses with these bright colors and mosaics. She wanted to be an architect when she grew up.

"Well, I like hamburgers," said Grant. Waving his money like a flag, he sped off toward The Grill.

Papa always ate soup. Mimi was a chocoholic. Soon, they had all gathered back at the table with their lunches. Papa stuck his hat back on his head and dished out the handful of napkins he had grabbed.

"Uh, Mimi?" said Grant. "Didn't you forget something?"

Mimi looked down at her tray. "I don't think so," she said. "Like what?"

Grant giggled. "Like to eat your lunch before you eat your dessert?"

Christina giggled too. Mimi had selected a big brownie and a cup of coffee. "Mimi, you would not get away with that at our school!" she teased her grandmother.

Mimi blushed. "Well, in this situation..." She looked at her watch. "Since it's only ten o'clock in the morning, I thought I could just enjoy a coffee break...and eat lunch later?"

Papa laughed. "Of course you can," he said, patting Mimi's hand. The kids giggled again. They knew that if Mimi came back to the food court, she would have her eye on more coffee and something else chocolate, and say, "I'll eat salad for supper."

"Uh, Mimi?" Christina said. "Could you please not use the word *situation?*"

Mimi looked confused. "Why?" she asked her granddaughter. "What's wrong with the word situation?"

Before Christina could answer, the nice man who had helped her and Grant earlier that morning walked briskly up to their table. "Good morning, again," he said hurriedly to the two kids.   Then he leaned down and whispered something in Mimi's ear. Papa looked surprised.

Mimi's eyes got very big.   Her eyelashes stood up like little exclamation points. "Oh my goodness," she said to the nice man. "Now that really is quite a SITUATION!"

Christina gasped. Grant kept chewing on his hamburger. Papa introduced himself to the nice man, and Mimi said, "Oh, I'm so sorry!   I've forgotten my manners. Everyone, please meet Mr. Bernie Marcus. THIS," she added, waving her brownie all around to indicate everything in sight, "is HIS AQUARIUM!"

A Gift for Atlanta

"Howdy!" said Papa, standing up and shaking Mr. Marcus's hand.

"What?" Christina said. "You didn't tell me this was your aquarium...sir," she added politely.

Even though Mr. Marcus acted like he was in a big hurry, he pulled out a peach-colored chair and sat down. "It isn't really my aquarium," he said, with a smile to Mimi. "The aquarium is the gift of my wife, Billi, and I to the city of Atlanta. We wanted kids just like you to enjoy it and learn about the sea and its creatures."

"Thanks," said Grant, as he continued to chew. Ketchup dripped down each side of his mouth to his chin. He looked like a little vampire or a very hungry shark.

Mimi gave Grant her famous "look."

"Oh, excuse me," Grant said immediately. "What I really meant to say was THANK YOU, SIR!"

Mr. Marcus laughed in spite of himself. He looked at Mimi and Papa. "I have grandkids, too," he noted. Then he said to Grant and Christina. "You're welcome!" Next he stood up and said, "And now I need you to go and enjoy the aquarium, while your grandmother comes with me, please." He looked at Papa who nodded in agreement.

Mimi stood up quickly and gave Papa a quick kiss on the cheek. "I'll meet up with you soon," she promised.

"I'll ride herd on these two," Papa promised her.

Christina couldn't help herself. No one usually came up to her grandmother (except to get her to autograph one of her mystery books) unless they needed her help with a mystery of some sort. But what kind of mystery could there be at a brand new aquarium that had just barely opened? She looked at Mr. Marcus and asked in a loud whisper, "Is it about the SITUATION?"

Mr. Marcus stooped down and looked Christina in the eye. "Young lady," he said gently, "what situation?" And then he and Mimi scooted out of the food court and across the atrium faster than a school of fish.

"Something very fishy is going on," Christina said to Papa.

"Now you know you need to stay out of it," her grandfather warned her. "You, too, sport," he reminded Grant.

"But when has Mimi ever solved a mystery lately without our help?" Christina asked with a big sigh.

"Yeah," added Grant. "Sheth neeth ouar hepth."

"What??" Papa and Christina asked together.

At last, Grant swallowed the food in his mouth. "I said: She needs our help!"

"Oh, no, she doesn't!" Papa warned them. "Now I'm going to sit here and take a quick siesta," he said, pulling his hat down over his eyes, "while you guys finish your breakfast, or lunch, or whatever it is we're having."

Papa always took a "quick siesta" after most meals. And when he was still softly snoring after Christina and Grant quickly gobbled down their food, they made a "management decision." They wrote Papa a BE BACK SOON note—and quietly scampered off to see if they could figure out:

    1. Just what the SITUATION was.

    2. If there really was a mystery.

    3. And how they might help solve it, or better yet, solve it before Mimi did!

7

A White Sport Coat and a Pink Crustacean

"Did you see where Mimi and Mr. Marcus went?" Grant asked his sister as they stood in the center of the atrium.

Christina couldn't get over the feeling of being inside a large arcade, with all the music, and lights, and video screens, and bright signs beckoning them to various areas of the aquarium.

"No," she finally answered her brother. "I guess we don't have any choice but to start looking through all the galleries until we find them. We can look at the fish and other animals as we go along," she added.

"Ok, then," Grant said. "But I came to see the aquarium, not solve some dumb old mystery."

Christina put her hands on her hips. "But Grant," she said, "what if it's a big mystery and important and fish—maybe even Norton and Ralph—are in danger?"

"Christina," Grant said, looking up at his sister. He put his hands on his hips. "Your imagination is too big for your britches!"

"Maybe so," Christina huffed. "But you can go back and sit with Papa if you want to."

"No way!" cried Grant. "I'm going to see all of the 100,000 little and big fishes in this aquarium...and solve a mystery, too, if we have to," he said.

Christina spun around. "Well, which way should we go first?"

Grant had no doubt. He pointed to a large entranceway made of rocks and waterfalls. "Let's head for River Scout. See—it says Freshwater Mysteries. That might be as good a place to start as any?"

Christina agreed and galloped after her brother who had already headed toward the gallery entrance.

Right from the start, the River Scout area captured their imaginations. Immediately, she and Grant started checking out fish from the rivers of Africa, South America, and Asia.

Christina loved the mysterious displays of masks and drums and the junglelike feel of the plants and waterfalls.

"Hey, look up!" Grant cried suddenly.

When Christina did, she was startled to see a river meandering over their heads. A glass ceiling let them look up at a river as if they were a bottom-feeding fish. Because she was staring upwards, she bumped right into the back of another visitor. He looked like a college medical student. He had on a grungy tee shirt beneath a white lab coat. He wore a backpack that he grabbed as if to protect it when Christina slammed into him.

The backpack was hard and Christina had the air jolted out of her lungs. Now I know how a fish out of water feels, she thought. She caught her breath and said, "Sorry!"

At first the boy just scowled at her, then he gave her a sort of "that's ok, don't worry about it" smile, and scurried away. Something about him bothered Christina but she didn't know what. She shrugged her shoulders, vowed to watch where she was going, then ran on ahead to catch up with Grant.

Grant was standing in front of a large tank filled with fish like they had never seen before. He was asking an aquarium staffer, "Can that fish really jump up into a tree an grab an insect to eat?"

"Sure can," the staffer told him. "Watch, I'll show you!"

Grant jumped back and Christina wondered if the fish was going to jump out of the tank into their laps! But then they saw that a monitor overhead was showing the Arawana swimming in a real-life river. As they gaped at the screen, all the visitors gathered around saw the fish jump right up out of the water and try to grab an insect from the trunk of a tree. It was amazing!

"Aha!" said Christina, "he jumped but he didn't get his snack."

Then she and Grant spied the insect, which had fallen in the water, where the fish snapped it up in its jaws.

"Oops," said Grant. "I actually think he did!"

Just then the overhead monitor got all staticy.

The aquarium staffer tapped it on the side, but it didn't help. "Shouldn't be doing that," he said to no one in particular.

"New computer stuff always has glitches," Christina said. "That's what my Uncle Michael always says."

"But this has been checked and rechecked," said the staffer, tapping the monitor once more. The monitor went blank. "Guess I'd better go check again," he said, with a frown, and jostled his way through the crowd to an exit.

Christina and Grant continued through the gallery exhibit.

"Well, I haven't seen anything mysterious here, have you?" Grant asked her, when they got to the end.

"No," Christina admitted, "just that weird fish and a messed-up monitor. Oh, and a grumpy guy I bumped into."

"Well, this looks sort of suspicious, I guess," Grant said. He stooped down and picked up a small, wadded rag from the floor. It had been tucked or shoved beneath the edge of a fake rock.

"What is it?" asked Christina.

"It's just an old rag," Grant said, opening his

hand to show her. Just then the rag moved, and much to the kids' surprise—out crawled...a hermit crab!

8

Cold Water Quest

"What in the world?!" Christina squealed.

Grant chuckled. "Aw, it's just a cute, little, old hermit crab. They move from shell to shell as they grow up, you know. I wish Mom would let me keep one as a pet."

"But what's it doing here?" asked Christina. She looked around. "There's no touch tank here, and this thing didn't crawl out of one, I don't think."

"It's not a thing," Grant insisted. "It's a hermit crab. But, no, I don't think it could crawl out of a tank, so it must have gotten here some other way."

Christina surprised herself by reaching out

and gently touching the shell. The legs within wiggled, giving her a start. "Cute," she said.

"They are cute," said Grant. "Good thing they can live out of water, but he'll need a drink soon."

"How do you know it's a he?" asked his sister.

"Cause I already named him Fred," Grant shot back.

Christina shook her head. "Ok. No time to argue, anyway. I think this sort of qualifies as a mystery...even if a little mystery, but I doubt it qualifies as a situation, much less a SITUATION, like Mimi and Mr. Marcus were talking about.

"Uh," said Grant, looking nervous. "This might count as a SITUATION for us," he warned, looking up.

Standing over them was a very big and tall aquarium staffer. She frowned. "And just what do you have there, kids?" she asked in a stern voice.

"A hermit crab!" Grant said cheerily, holding the critter up for her to see.

"I can see that," said the staffer. "But exactly where did you get it?"

"We found it," Christina spurted. "Right here. Just now. No idea how it got here."

The staffer leaned down. "Well I think I'd better get the little guy back into a tank," she said. "You know," she added in a serious tone, "the touch tanks are for touching...not taking." Gently, she plucked the hermit crab from Grant's palm.

Christina blushed. She felt like she might cry. She sure didn't want anyone thinking that she or Grant would steal a hermit crab or do anything to hurt any of the creatures in the aquarium. Grant must have felt the same way because he folded his arms and tucked his fists into his sides the way he did when he was angry.

"We found him!" Grant protested.

"Really!" Christina added. "Someone must have brought the hermit crab in with them."

The staffer looked aggravated, but she smiled anyway. "Why don't you kids find your parents and go back to enjoying the aquarium," she said as she turned and walked off.

"But it's true!" Christina cried after her. "We promise!!"

The staffer just glanced back and kept going. Christina and Grant sat in the floor, dejected. "Boy, if Mimi or Papa hear we've taken a fish out of water—even if we didn't—we'll be deep-sixed forever!" Grant said.

Christina stood up and dusted herself off. "No we won't!" she retorted.

"Why not?" asked Grant, looking very puzzled. He stood up too.

"Because," Christina said with a determined voice, "they'll believe us." Her feelings were hurt and so was her pride. Besides, the staffer had just taken their first real clue. And any good mystery-solver knew you needed all the clues you could find to solve a mystery—even if everyone else was determined to call the mystery a SITUATION.

"Come on, Grant," Christina said, tugging her brother by his shirtsleeve. "Let's go right next door to the next gallery and continue our search. It will help me cool off. I'm sort of hot under the collar."

"It is sort of warm in here," Grant agreed, as he followed his sister. "But how will this gallery cool you...OH!" he said suddenly. "I see!" Grant looked up at the attractive and inviting entrance to COLD WATER QUEST: The Chilly Unknown. "Cool!" he said. "Let's go!"

As they exited the gallery, Grant spotted a tank of piranha and said, "Hey, Christina, here's a touch tank...stick your hand in."

Christina just glared at her brother. "I know a little brother who needs tossing to the piranha!" she said and grabbed at Grant.

Grant laughed, pulled away, and dashed right into the next gallery past the ice and snow-covered rock entrance. Christina took her time. She was going to look closely at everything. If there were clues to be found, she would find them. And she wasn't going to be blamed for something that she hadn't done—it was insulting.

It was interesting to see sea creatures that lived in a cold water environment, Christina thought. She was more familiar with the warm water fish and crabs and other critters that lived on the coast.

While Grant bounced from tank to tank ahead of her, until she could no longer see him, Christina tagged along behind one of the aquarium staffers who was leading a small tour.

"The animals in this gallery give you a glimpse of the rich variety of life found in cold ocean waters," the staffer explained. "These areas have some of the largest fisheries in the world. Unfortunately, many of these cold water creatures are in peril."

"What can we do?" one concerned visitor asked.

The staffer stroked his chin. "We need to manage our ocean resources better," he said. "Only if we protect our marine life can we be sure that there will be fisheries in the future."

Christina looked at all the beautiful (and some funky-looking!) fish she saw in the tanks before her. It would be such a waste for any of these amazing creatures to be threatened with extinction. She had helped in one of the turtle-saving programs on the coast one year with Mimi and Papa. It had made her realize how fragile beach and wetland and ocean habitats were...as well as the creatures that called these places home. Hmm, she thought, maybe I'll grow up and become a marine biologist.

As she ogled the fish and daydreamed, the tour went on. Up ahead, she heard an out-of-tune voice singing, "You otter be in pictures! You otter be a star!"

Grant! Christina scampered ahead and, sure enough, there was her little brother singing at the top of his lungs to the funny sea otters. They swam on their backs while they played with small toys. It was hard to tell who looked happier—

Grant, the otters, or the amused tourists. After all, Grant only knew how to sing while he was also dancing. And his dancing was as silly as his singing!

"Hey, Grant," Christina cried, catching up to him. "Pipe down. Maybe the otters prefer to be the ones to do the entertaining. You know what I mean?"

Her brother was undaunted. "I OTTER BE IN PICTURES!" he sang. "I OTTER BE A STAAAAAAAR!"

Christina blushed. Little brothers! She reached forward to grab Grant by the sleeve and pull him away from the tank. Just then, Christina spied the kid in the lab coat frowning at them. As she and Grant moved on to the next exhibit, she heard the boy hiss, "Leave the poor animals alone." Something in the tone of his voice gave Christina a cold chill. Or perhaps, she wondered, it was just cooler in this part of the aquarium?

Christina shook the feeling off. She reminded herself that she and Grant were on a quest for clues as to the SITUATION. So far, she thought, no luck. Of course it would help if they had an idea what the mysterious SITUATION was.

Before she could sit Grant down on one of the

benches conveniently located around the aquarium and remind him of their mission, he called out to her.

"Come look at this!" he said.

When Christina caught up, she saw one of her favorite animals—penguins! Loads of them were prancing across rocks and plunging into the water. They would swim quickly to the other side of the tank, scamper ashore, then start their trek once more. They were so funny and cute!

Grant grinned and pointed to a sign. "They're called Jackass Penguins!" he said.

"I don't think you're supposed to say that word," Christina admonished her brother. "You'd better not let Papa hear you!"

"What?" asked Grant, "Penguins? I can't say penguins?!"

"No!" said Christina. Then she sighed and muttered, "Nevermind."

"Nevermind about what?" a voice behind them said, surprising both kids.

Christina and Grant whipped around. "Mimi!" Christina said. "Where have you been?"

"I was going to ask you two the same question," Mimi said. "I just met up with your grandfather and he's been looking all over for you."

"He was taking one of his little cat naps," explained Christina. "We didn't want to wake him, so I guess we just couldn't resist and wandered off to look at fish."

Mimi laughed. "I understand that!" she said. "It's hard not to want to look and see everything in this place all at the same time."

Christina couldn't help herself...she jumped right to the question burning a hole in her head. "What's the SITUATION, Mimi?"

Her grandmother sighed. "Let's go sit over here," she whispered. Eagerly, Christina followed her to a bench near the penguin exhibit. Grant was busy poking his head up in a special tunnel in the exhibit where you could get face-to-face with the penguins. Both Christina and Mimi laughed at Grant making faces at the penguins. The more the penguins ignored him, the weirder faces Grant made.

"It's hard to tell which is the Jackass Penguin, isn't it?" Mimi whispered to Christina with a giggle.

Christina giggled back. "That's silly, Mimi!"

"Silly...but true!" Mimi said, totally entertained by her grandson's antics. Then she turned serious. "But what's not silly is this SITUATION, as you call it. Really, no one knows what to make of it."

"Make of what?" Christina asked eagerly. Sometimes her grandmother just didn't make sense. It was so exasperating!

Mimi lowered her voice even further and turned to look around as if to be sure they weren't being followed or watched. Her actions gave Christina an eerie feeling. "Well," said Mimi, "keep this under your hat, but strange, unexplainable things have been happening in the aquarium since it opened. Nothing really bad so far, but there is so much security that none of the staff can figure out how anything is happening. Maybe it's just opening day glitches...or..."

"Or what?" Christina begged.

Mimi had worry lines around her eyes and mouth. She acted like she had not heard Christina's question. Christina knew this was how her grandmother acted when she was trying to solve a mystery...she kept thinking out loud and talking mostly to herself until her mind bumped into a clue or an idea of what was going wrong and how to solve it.

"Or what?" Christina repeated with more urgency.

Mimi got quiet then finally said, "Or if things get worse, they might have to close the aquarium, and that would be such a shame since it's so wonderful, and everyone has worked so hard, and..."

Christina interrupted her grandmother. "Close the aquarium?!" she whispered more loudly than she should have. "The SITUATION can't be that bad?"

Mimi frowned and shook her head. "Not yet, perhaps," she said. "But..."

Before Mimi could finish her sentence, she was interrupted again—this time by a giant howl of "WOW!!!!!!!"

"Grant," said Mimi, shaking her head.

Christina shook her head too. "GRANT!"

Armed...
and Dangerous?

Christina and her grandmother jumped up off the bench and hurried to the next exhibit. There stood Grant in front of a dark tank. At first all they could see was the dark water. Then they spotted a wad of orange...a very large wad of orange. The wad of orange suddenly spewed out arms...lots and lots of arms.

"An octopus!" Mimi said with delight.

Grant turned. His eyes were big with wonder. "No, Mimi!" he said. "Count them... oneapus...twoapus...threeapus...fourapus ...fiveapus...sixapus...sevenapus—it only has seven arms! An octopus is supposed to have eight arms, right?"

"Right!" said a deep voice and they all turned to look at Mr. Marcus who was watching the octopus fondly. "An octopus usually does have eight arms," he agreed. "But Taco is a giant Pacific Coast octopus who probably had his arm bitten off when he was young. However, if you look closely, you can see an arm bud—he's growing a new arm!"

"Wow!" said Grant, kneeling down in front of the tank to better examine the octopus. "That's really neat."

Mr. Marcus smiled. "So, yes, right now Taco is indeed a sevenapus, as you call it, but one day, he'll be a full-fledged eight-tentacled octopus again."

Christina was fascinated. But she was also afraid. "Aren't octopuses or octopi or whatever you call a lot of them...dangerous?" She was eyeing the big, fat suckers on the octopus's arms. Each of the suction cups looked like they could do some serious harm if they got hold of you, she thought.

"If you learn about octopus, or octopi," Mr. Marcus began, "you will learn that they are very smart. You might say that they are the gifted and talented creatures of the sea! They like to figure things out. That's why we hide some of their food in those tubes," he added, pointing to four-inch wide white plastic pipes with holes in them. Taco was slipping an arm into the pipe. The tip of the tentacle explored each hole searching for food. When it found a shrimp, it grabbed it and slid its tentacle back out of the pipe and into its beak.

"So, yes," Mr. Marcus continued. "An octopus is a predator, but if you don't bother it, it probably won't bother you!"

Don't worry about that, Christina thought to herself.

Mr. Marcus surprised all the listeners who had gathered around by saying, "And an octopus is a very social creature. It likes to play. It likes to be touched and to touch—any volunteers?"

Christina cringed and backed away. Grant threw up both of his hands.

Mr. Marcus laughed. "Young man," he said to Grant, "I think you have the makings of an aquarist!"

"A whatist?" asked Grant.

Mimi had come forward. She put her arm around her grandson's shoulder. "An aquarium worker," she said. "If you go to college and study hard, you can work in a variety of jobs at an aquarium."

Christina had backed further away and sat down on the bench. Oh, great, she thought. Grant acts silly and he gets to be an aquarist. I'm the one who wants to be a marine biologist.

"So I could be a octopus hugger?" Grant asked happily.

Both Mimi and Mr. Marcus laughed.

"You can be anything you want to be, Grant!" Mr. Marcus said.

Christina was like her grandmother—very observant. So, she didn't miss the curious look Mr. Marcus gave Mimi. It was easy to translate: Let's get back to the SITUATION. Christina could tell by the look in Mr. Marcus's eyes that either the situation was getting more serious or something else had happened.

Still, Mr. Marcus just smiled at the crowd. "Everyone watch the monitor," he suggested, pointing to the screen over his head, "and you'll learn even more about the Pacific octopus who now makes his home in our wonderful new aquarium."

From somewhere behind her, Christina heard a voice hiss, "Fish prison! An aquarium is a fish prison!"

She felt sure that the voice sounded familiar. She spun around, expecting to see the weird boy in the lab coat, but she only saw an aquarium staffer with his arms folded, leaning against the wall. When she turned back to tell Mimi and Mr. Marcus—they were gone!

Papa in Pink!

Just as Christina and Grant prepared to move on through the Cold Water Quest exhibit, she noticed that the monitor began to mess up. There was a lot of static and white lines and spots. That seems curious, she thought to herself. I'm sure they have lots of computer nerds around here like her Uncle Michael who was a real "digital guru," according to Mimi.

"C'mon, Christina!" Grant urged his sister. "I think we can solve the mystery if we look at more fish."

Christina smiled. She knew Grant was a lot more interested in the fascinating array of fish in the aquarium than he was in a mystery that he couldn't understand. She couldn't blame him. She would much rather just enjoy the aquarium experience than stew over some stupid mystery—wouldn't she? Secretly, Christina suspected that she might grow up and be a mystery writer, like her grandmother, someday. She was good at writing, had a vivid imagination, and loved to read. She just had to work harder on her spelling and her grammar.

As usual, Christina was thinking so hard that she forgot where she was going. Suddenly, she followed Grant around a corner made of what looked like fake stone and gasped. Or maybe, she thought later, she should have "Gaspered?"

In front of her was one of the most magical things she had ever seen—a big, giant ghost! Really, it was a baby beluga whale. It was snow white. It looked soft and round and curvy, truly like a ghost or a stuffed animal shape. She just wanted to give it a big hug! Best of all, the beluga had a mouth in the shape of a smile. It made her smile.

Not surprisingly, Grant was glued to the side of the tank like one of those sticky frogs. His forehead, nose, hands and knees were smashed against the glass.

"Loooooooooooooooooook!" he whispered to his sister. "Am I imagining things?"

Christina put her arm around his shoulders. "No, you're not," she promised. For a long time, they just stood there and watched in awe. There were plenty of adults and kids around, but they too were completely quiet, watching the baby beluga whale dart and swerve, sway and dip. He (or she?) came right up to the window and seemed to look them all directly in the eye with his (her?) big, black eye. Then the whale surprised everyone by popping its head up out of the water and spewing a burst of water into the air!

But Grant was not surprised. "That's how mammals breathe," he said, mostly to himself. Then he added another, "Loooooooooooooook!"

They read that this tank held 800,000 gallons of water. Beluga whales normally live in Arctic waters as cold as 32 degrees. Freezing, Christina thought. They grow ten to fifteen feet long and weigh around 3,000 pounds. Fish, squid, crabs, and clams are what they love to eat.

Suddenly, from around a hidden corner of the tank swam another beluga. Then another. And another. Another. And another!

"Five!" Christina cried. Everyone around the tank was *oohing* and *aahing*.

After watching the pod of whales cavort for a while, Christina got absorbed by the video monitor. It described how Gasper and Nico, two of the whales, had been rescued from a pond beneath a rollercoaster in an amusement park. The pond was small and the coaster noisy. The whales had been sickly. They had scars on their skin and other problems.

"Look how those people got right in the water to help them," Grant said. "I think it would be fun to be a fishanarium or an aquarinarium or..."

"I think it's just a veterinarium," Christina guessed.

Then they learned that the other whales had come from a pond beneath a different rollercoaster. That seemed curious to Christina. So did the fact that they had had to load Gasper and Nico on a kiddie train to get them out of the amusement park so they could come to this aquarium on a UPS airplane.

"Where there's a will there's a way," said a deep voice behind them

"Papa!" both kids shrieked. "Where have you been?"

Their grandfather put his arms around both

of their shoulders. "I think the important question is: Where have you kids been?"

Christina squirmed. "Just looking around," she said. "We knew you'd catch up with us."

"I usually do," Papa reminded her with a grin.

"Yeah, and that's when I usually end up in Time Out!" complained Grant.

"TIME OUT!" Christina cried suddenly.

"Yeah, that's what I said," said Grant.

"No, I mean look!" squealed Christina.

Grant and Papa looked up to see what Christina was talking about. At first they didn't understand. Then they gasped. The beluga tank water was turning pink, then pinker. It looked like the snow white whales were turning the color of peppermint.

"What's happening?" Papa asked gruffly. "This can't be right."

"Maybe it's food, or medicine," Christina suggested, hopefully.

"It makes me think of cotton candy," said Grant.

The whales did not seem to mind, but the visitors first talked in hushed tones, then louder, wondering what was going on.

Finally, an aquarium staffer overheard the

ruckus and ran up to the tank. The visitors looked at her, expecting an explanation. Instead the woman slapped her hands to her cheeks. "OHMYGOSH!" she hollered and ran off.

In a minute, several security officers appeared. They escorted the visitors, including Christina, Grant, and Papa, to the exit.

"This exhibit is temporarily closed, folks," one said. "So sorry. Perhaps you'll be able to return shortly."

Christina felt like she was getting the "bum's rush," as Papa called it. She really didn't want to leave. She glanced quickly back over her shoulder and saw the whales still swimming leisurely in their new tank home. "It looks like a Nutcracker ballet!" she muttered to herself.

"What?" asked Papa, leading them to a bench in the hallway.

"I think I know what nut did this," Grant grumbled.

"What?!" said Papa, sitting down.

"Hush, Grant," his sister urged.

"Christina?" Papa said. His cheeks were bright pink. As pink as the beluga tank water. He gave her the look that meant "tell me what's going on."

Christina plopped down on the bench between her grandfather and her brother.

"Christina..." Papa repeated. "Fess up! What do you know about this...this...SITUATION?"

"Oh, no," moaned Grant. "the S-word!"

11

Jelly Belly

Christina sighed. "Really, Papa, not much. We actually don't know much at all. We saw Mimi and Mr. Marcus a few minutes ago. They mentioned the SITUATION, but I still don't know what that means."

Papa patted Christina on the head. "Well maybe you aren't supposed to, young lady," he said. "We brought you to the aquarium to have fun and learn a fish thing or two, you know—not to solve a mystery...especially one that might not even exist!"

Christina plopped her chin in her hands. "I know," she said, "but you know I can't resist! Besides, we saw some things."

"Like what?" Papa asked. "What kind of things?"

"Like a suspicious kid in a lab coat," said Grant. "And the monitors got all messed up. And you saw that pink stuff in the fish tank."

Papa shoved his cowboy hat back on his head and sighed. "Well none of that sounds too suspicious to me. It's opening day. There is bound to be a glitch or two. Nothing to worry about."

Papa tapped his cowboy boot heels impatiently. He never liked to sit still for long. "I think I'll go see how we get our Annual Pass badges," he said, standing up and stretching. "Why don't you two just relax." He looked across the atrium and pointed to a sign. "Try that gallery!"

Christina and Grant looked to where their grandfather was pointing. It was the Tropical Diver gallery. The Coral Kingdom the sign read.

"Sure!" said Grant, ready to see some more fish.

"Oh, all right," Christina agreed. She tried to act nonchalant, but secretly she was glad that she and Grant were getting to go off on their own again. After all, that would be a new gallery to explore and maybe they would pick up more clues.

As they entered the gallery, Christina had a curious feeling...and it was totally unrelated to the mystery. It was far more related to the mystery of the sea. She and Grant were mesmerized by the sea sights before them. Christina realized that all the visitors were totally captivated as a hush descended over the crowd which mostly just stood around and stared, their mouths often gaping open at the seahorses, squid, and jawfish.

Even Grant was caught up in the drama of the scenes. "Look," he whispered softly to his sister, "jellyfish...lots and lots of them."

Sure enough, right in front of their eyes, bulbous, glistening, pulsating jellyfish moved through the water like pale little moons or hot air balloons.

Christina couldn't help but think that many of the fish they saw were like colorful jewels. Mimi has necklaces this bright, she thought to herself. There must be more colors than I can name. And speaking of names, Christina loved to see and read about sea creatures with names like the Mandarin fish that looked like a living kaleidoscope, or the Clown triggerfish, whose funny shape and colors made you laugh out loud.

But Christina hadn't seen anything yet! Once more, as she and Grant wound through the dark corridors, they came across a scene completely unexpected. Without a word—not even the GASP! they felt inside—they plunked down on the carpet in front of a gigantic tank window. Inside was one of the most beautiful things Christina thought she had ever seen—a living coral reef!

From right in front of their faces to high over their heads hovered a wall of colorful coral arrayed like the window of a florist's shop. In and among and around all the coral, spit and swirled and moseyed and scooted fish in as many colors as the rainbow.

"Have you ever seen a blue that bright?" Christina finally asked her brother. She pointed to a fish in a color that she could only describe as electric blue.

"Look at that gold one!" said Grant. "It's golder than gold. It almost hurts my eyes to look at the silly thing. And I really like all the flowers."

Christina laughed. "Those aren't flowers, Grant," she said. "Those are sea creatures too."

"Wow!" said Grant. "Who woulda thunk it?"

"Papa says a coral reef is a very fragile environment...that you can kill it with pollution."

"Then I guess that stuff can't be very good for this reef," groused Grant. He pointed up near the top of the tank. When Christina looked, she could see some items floating down through the water. A few fish swam up to them, then ignored them and swam away.

There was a buzz of conversation as visitors watched the items glide to the bottom of the tank. They finally fell to the sand just in front of Grant and Christina.

"Hmm," said Christina. "Plastic junk!" She pointed at a plastic toy scuba diver, a small rubber ball, what looked like bottle caps, and more.

"Are those toys for the fish to play with?" Grant asked with a skeptical tone in his voice.

"I think someone is trying to sabotage the coral reef tank," Christina guessed. "Probably our white lab coat friend."

"He's not our friend," Grant argued.

"That's just a figure of speech, Grant," Christina explained. "You know, I was so captivated by the coral reef that I almost forgot about the SITUATION. I don't think Mimi and

Mr. Marcus are making much progress, or this wouldn't have happened."

Suddenly there was a louder conversation behind them. Christina and Grant turned to see an aquarium staffer and a man in a suit discussing something and pointing to the reef tank.

"Looks like this act of vandalism's been discovered," said Christina. "Come on, Grant, let's get out of here and get back to mystery-solving before something even worse happens."

"What could be worse?" asked Grant as he followed his sister.

Grant didn't want to know.

12

Fish Food

As Christina and Grant quickly exited the Tropical Diver gallery, they ran smack into Papa. "Hey!" he said with excitement. "I've arranged for us to have a great tour of some parts of the aquarium most visitors don't get to see."

Papa was good (he always said) at finagling neat "tours" for them to go on. Christina thought it was because her grandfather was so jovial and friendly. Mimi said it was because Papa just wouldn't take no for an answer. Either way, if Papa cooked up some special behind-the-scenes tour, it was usually a treat.

However, this time Christina was far more eager to pursue the mystery than she was to take any tour. Of course, she couldn't exactly tell

Papa that without admitting that she and Grant were still secretly working on the "off limits" SITUATION.   Besides, Papa was already shuttling them to an elevator where a smiling aquarium staffer waited for them.

"Where are we going?" asked Grant. He was always in favor of getting into places most people weren't supposed to go. Unfortunately, that often meant disappearing through secret doorways (like at the Biltmore House), falling into the San Antonio River when they visited the Alamo, or "accidentally" taking off on a hang glider in a hurricane when they were at Kill Devil Hills.

"I'm taking you to see the gourmet food preparation area," said the staffer.

"Oh," said Grant in disappointment. "You mean like where they make food for the aquarium cafeteria?"

The staffer laughed. "No, I mean where we make food for the fish."

"Fish food?" said Christina. "Don't you just shake it out of a big box? Or toss the fish some, I don't know, eels or something?"

The staffer shook his head. "Oh no," he said. "Feeding fish to keep them healthy and happy is quite a job. It's a real combination of good food and good science."

"Good grief," said Papa. "I thought fish just ate...smaller fish," he teased.

The staffer opened the elevator door and cleared his throat. "Not in our aquarium!" he assured them.

When they stepped off the elevator into what looked like a laboratory, Christina got excited. People were working hard at their tasks; many wore lab coats. She winked at Grant and they both looked around hurriedly, but they did not spy the guy they were so suspicious of.

"I can see you two are excited," said Papa. "Aren't you glad I arranged this little behind-the-scenes adventure?"

Christina frowned. "Sure, Papa. It smells so, uh, delicious in here."

Grant looked puzzled. He wrinkled his freckled nose. "I think it smells FISHY!" he complained.

"Well I should hope so," said the staffer. "But this is not ordinary fish food—this is pretty gourmet stuff. Come take a look."

The stainless steel room had a freezer that could hold 20,000 pounds of food and keep it frozen at minus twenty degrees Fahrenheit. A large refrigerator could hold 6,000 pounds of frozen fish food.

The staffer lead them to an area where great batches of krill (small shrimp) were being mixed with nutritious vitamins. "This is Ralph's and Norton's favorite food."

Grant leaned over the mixture, then stuck his finger in his throat and pretended to gag. "Yummy!" he said. "I think I'll order a supersize bowl."

Papa inhaled deeply and smiled. Christina laughed. Her grandfather loved seafood, but *really*, she thought.

"I guess you have to make a lot of fish food for the whale sharks?" Christina guessed.

"Oh, yes," said the staffer. "They each eat—well, inhale actually—about 34 pounds of krill each day.

"Boy," said Grant. "Mimi would not like to cook for them!"

As they watched the operation, Christina noticed that two of the men in lab coats began to whisper in an animated and serious discussion.

"No way!" she overheard one man say.

"Well, what else could it be?" the other

man said.

"Is anything wrong?" asked Papa, who was never shy about butting into anyone's business.

"Uh, no," said one of the men. He looked surprised to see that they had been overheard. But when the staffer led them past the men to another area, Christina heard the other man say, "This batch is tainted. It would make the fish sick. It just isn't possible!"

Christina hung back as long as she could, until Papa turned and urged her to catch up with them.

"Come on," said the staffer. "They're about to feed Ralph and Norton. You might as well take a peek. It's something to see!"

Uh, oh, Christina thought. "Are they going to feed them this batch?" she asked in fear.

The staffer looked puzzled. "No," he said. "There is already a batch made for them." He looked at Christina curiously, then shrugged his shoulders and turned, indicating that they should follow him.

When they got to the feeding area, Christina and Grant were astounded. They realized that they were standing at the top of the giant tank where Ralph and Norton swam.

"This is HUGE!" Christina cried.

"Aw, it's bigger than that," said Grant in amazement.

The staffer laughed. "Yes, it's pretty awesome to see this for the first time."

Christina looked around. The gigantic tank looked about the size of a football field to her. Built across it was what Papa called a "catwalk." It was a narrow bridge.

"Well," said the staffer, "are you ready to feed Ralph and Norton?"

"Really?" asked Grant.

"Truly?" asked Christina.

"Can I come too?" Papa asked eagerly. He and Mimi were really fourth-graders at heart and never wanted to miss out on anything.

"Sure," said the staffer. "But watch your step and follow the feeder's rules, please."

Christina shivered with excitement. She had never stood on top of an aquarium tank that looked as big as a lake...or fed giant fish...especially not fish with the word "shark" as part of their name.

Carefully, Grant, then Christina, then Papa,

then the staffer walked out onto the catwalk. A feeder in a white lab coat was leaning over the catwalk. His head was down over the water as he positioned the yellow and green scoops full of krill in the water.

When he nodded, Christina and Grant drew closer and watched as Ralph and Norton took turns coming up to get their food.

"Wow!" said Grant, "this is so cool. I wish I had an aquarium this big."

"And where would you put it?" asked Papa.

"Hey," said Grant. "Maybe in the neighborhood swimming pool?"

Christina laughed. "That would sure make summer swimming exciting!"

As Ralph and Norton finished eating and swept off into the deep water out of sight, the feeder began to draw in the long-handled scoops. He still did not look up or speak, but the staffer said, "Ok, folks, that's the show...let's get back to the side."

He turned and walked off with Papa following him. Then Christina turned and followed Papa. When they got back to the side of the tank, they turned and saw the feeder running off the other end of the catwalk, leaving the food bin and scoops behind. The man was peeling off his lab coat which he threw down as he disappeared through an EXIT door.

It was only then that Christina and Papa realized at the same time that GRANT WAS GONE!

A Swim with the Fishes

"GRANT! GRANT!! GRAAAAAAAAANT!" Christina and her grandfather screamed together. They ran back and forth across the catwalk peering down into the water, but they could see nothing.

"Maybe he left through the EXIT door," said the staffer. "Maybe the feeder went after him."

"And maybe the feeder shoved my little brother overboard!" Christina screeched. She thought she was going to cry. Grant was a good swimmer, but this was a lot of deep water—full of fish!

Without thinking or speaking, Christina

dashed for the stairs and flew down and down and down to the main level of the aquarium. As fast as she could run, she pushed visitors aside as she dashed through the dim corridors to the big tank. A scuba diver was down in the tank. She waved at the crowd.

"Maybe she can save Grant," Christina turned to say to Papa. But Papa had not followed her. Now she had lost Grant and Papa!

Christina thought hard...what to do now? Suddenly, she heard Mimi's voice behind her.

"Hey, girlie," said Mimi. "I thought we could have a snack in the cafeteria."

With dread, Christina turned and fell into her grandmother's arms. "What's wrong?" Mimi asked.

Christina looked up with big, wet eyes and tried to blubber all that had happened, but she could not get the words out right.

"What? What?" Mimi kept asking. Then suddenly, Mimi's eyes got big, then bigger. She was staring at the tank. Then she did something Christina had never heard her grandmother do before—she screamed at the top of her lungs!

Now everyone stared at the tank and gasped because coming into view behind the scuba diver was a small boy.

"GRAAAAAANT!" Christina and Mimi cried together. They ran up to the tank and pressed their hands on the glass.

Shockingly, Grant just gave them a tiny wave, then spread his arms and pushed up—with a whoosh of water and bubbles—and vanished.

"Christina! How did this happen?" Mimi asked. "How did he get in? How can he get out?" Mimi looked this way and that as if she did not know what to do.

Now it was Christina's turn to be shocked. PAPA APPEARED IN THE TANK! "Mimi, look!" she cried.

Mimi did look, and once more screamed at the top of her lungs: "GET OUT OF THERE! GET GRANT!! THERE ARE SHARKS IN THERE!!!"

"No, no, Mimi," Christina said. "They are named sharks, but they are just fish, Mimi. Papa and Grant will be ok."

"They're BIG FISH!" Mimi roared. She pointed to Papa who nodded and, like Grant, pushed up into the water and disappeared.

The scuba diver looked totally confused. All this had happened behind her and she could not imagine what the uproar from the crowd outside the tank was about. When she looked around behind her...there was nothing to see.

"Christina," said Mimi, grabbing her granddaughter by the arm, "Get me up there—now!"

"OK!" Christina shouted. She grabbed Mimi's hand. "Let's run!" she said, and she and her grandmother took off.

They arrived back upstairs just in time to see Grant and Papa emerge—soaking wet and dripping water everywhere—from the tank. Staffers helped pull them out of the water. Someone handed them each a towel.

"Well that was quite an adventure," said Papa, sputtering. He wiped his face and hair.

"Pffft! Pfffft!" sputtered Grant. "I think I ate some krill...or fish poop...or something."

In great relief, Mimi and Christina laughed. The foursome grabbed one another for big hugs, the girls not even caring if they got wet.

"I'm so relieved," said Mimi. "But what in the world happened? How did you end up in the tank?"

"Good thing I've been on the rec swim team practically since I was born," said Grant, as he continued to towel dry.

"Papa, you're a hero," said Christina. "You must have jumped right in after Grant."

"Of course!" boomed Papa. "And I wish you could have seen the look on your faces when you saw us in the water."

"I wish you could have seen the look on your own faces!" said Mimi. "But I still don't understand—why were you in the water in the first place?"

A very grim looking group of aquarium staffers and men in suits now stood nearby.

"That's exactly what we'd like to know," said one of them.

Everyone turned and looked at Grant. Grant turned beet red. "It wasn't my fault!" he swore. "That guy who was feeding Norton and Ralph...he pushed me!"

Mimi gasped. "And just why would he do that?" she asked. She was not looking at Grant...she was staring at the aquarium staff.

Before any of them could speak, Christina reluctantly piped up. "I think I might know," she squeaked.

Now all eyes were on her, her least favorite thing.

"And what does that mean?" demanded Mimi.

Christina gave a big sigh. "Remember the SITUATION we were not supposed to get involved in?"

Mimi nodded heartily. "Oh, I remember," she said.

"Well, we really didn't get involved," Christina promised and Grant nodded his spiky wet hair in agreement. "We just used our powers of observation. We kept seeing this guy—he looked sort of young—in a lab coat. He kept muttering ugly things. And when we saw some other things happen like the monitors mess up and the whale tank turn pink, and junk toys in the coral reef exhibit, we thought maybe he was up to something."

"Well why didn't you tell us?!" Mimi and Papa said together. The aquarium staff looked quite confused, as if these people were much stranger than any fish in the tanks.

"We wanted to," said Christina. "But every time I turned around you were gone. We thought if we kept our eyes open we might solve the mystery before the SITUATION got any worse."

One of the men in suits cleared his throat. "And so you think that the feeder was actually an imposter? That he was the same young man you saw earlier?"

Christina shrugged her shoulders. "I never saw his face," she said. "But Grant said he pushed him in the water...and then the guy ran off."

The men in the suits looked at the aquarium staffer who had been on duty when Ralph and Norton were fed. "The guy did run off," the staffer said. "It was pretty suspicious. So were some anomalies in the tests on the krill mixture, even though the food was perfectly fine."

"But who would want to hurt the nice fishies?" Grant asked. Now he looked like he might cry.

Suddenly, a door opened and into the room stepped a surprise visitor. "I think I can tell you why," he said.

"Please do!" begged Mimi.

14

Food for Thought

Mr. Marcus came up and joined the group. He shook his head sadly, but Christina could also tell he was aggravated.

"Unfortunately, some people do not understand the mission of aquariums," he explained. "They think it's bad that the fish are captured or taken out of the wild, and moved to tanks to live out their lives."

"What do the fish think?" asked Grant.

Mr. Marcus smiled. "I wish we knew!" he admitted. "But aquariums serve a great purpose. For one thing, when people see fish and other sea creatures that they may only read about, they realize how important it is to protect our seas and the life that lives there. Our whole goal is education. Plus, we also have saved many of our fish from a much worse situation. We make sick fish well again. And, we protect and pamper our fish here at the aquarium."

"Of course you do!" Mimi said. "Surely no one doubts that?"

"Well," said Mr. Marcus, "it seems that at least one person does."

Mr. Marcus was a man of decision and action. "Here's what we're going to do," he said with a twinkle in his eye. "That is if it's ok with you?" He looked at Mimi, Papa, Grant, and Christina one by one. They all nodded. The group huddled closer, and Mr. Marcus outlined his surprising plan.

Christina and Grant didn't mind the PLAN at all. For one thing, it required them to go with Mimi and Papa to see Deepo's Undersea 4-D Wondershow in the aquarium's special theater built just for what was said to be an amazing production.

Papa had tickets and they went and listened to a guy dressed as a funny professor who gave them a little lecture on fish. But Christina and Grant were more eager to get inside the theater and try out the special eyeglasses they had been given.

"I know what 3-D is," said Grant. "But what is 4-D?"

"I don't know," said Christina, "but I'm sure it will be cool."

"Not too cool, I hope," said Mimi, who did not like unexpected surprises in the dark.

"We can go in now," said Papa.

As they got settled in their seats, Christina said, "This seems like an ordinary theater to me." But as soon as the movie started, they realized that they were in for lots of surprises.

The 3-D included an exciting animated movie. With the glasses on, the fish in the story appeared to zoom out of the screen right in front of your face. Mimi squealed each time.

But more than that, in parts of the movie a fine mist of water sprayed down on you...magical lightning crackled overhead...fins from somewhere under your seat flapped your legs, and tentacles swept down from the ceiling.

"This is wild!" said Christina, when the movie was over.

"Boy, that was fun!" said Grant. "Let's watch it again!"

"I think I'm deaf," said Papa.

"I didn't scream that much, did I?" insisted Mimi.

Everyone leaving the theater wore a big grin. The movie was so exciting that Christina realized that she had forgotten all about the next phase in their attempt to solve the mystery.

As they exited the theater, they dropped their glasses in a collection bin. Then, according to the PLAN, they left the theater.

Mimi whispered, "Good luck!" and went in one direction.

Papa gave both kids a big wink and headed in another direction.

"Hey, Grant," Christina said loudly, standing at the top of the stairs. "Look at that big lighthouse over there. That's one gallery we haven't been to. Let's go check it out."

"You don't have to holler at me," Grant complained, looking at his sister like she was crazy. Then he remembered the PLAN. "Oh, yeah!" he said loudly. "I would like to go there. HERE WE GO!"

The two kids went down the staircase, looking neither left nor right nor behind them, just straight ahead. They took their time as they walked across the big open area at the bottom of the stairs. Although Christina felt a little nervous, she couldn't help but giggle as she and Grant paraded through the Discover Our Coast entranceway.

However, as usual, Grant had a mind of his own.

"Hey, Christina," he said, tugging at her sleeve. "Stop! Look! It's a touch tank." She spotted sea skates and sharks swirling around in the shallow water.

"Haven't you had enough up-close-and-personal encounters with fish for one day?" his sister asked. "Besides..."

But Grant was so eager to touch the sea creatures that he just ignored his sister. Soon, like many other kids, he was leaning over the touch tank gently stroking the horseshoe crabs, sea stars, stingrays, and shrimp.

While Grant did that, Christina looked around. She knew what the PLAN was, she just hoped that it worked. As she waited impatiently for Grant, she examined a tank of funny hermit crabs. She tried to spot the one that they had rescued, but could not. Then she took a glimpse of a film about northern right whales, the most endangered whale species on earth. Pretty soon, she realized that she had forgotten the time.

"C'mon, Grant!" she urged her brother.

Grumbling, Grant followed her to the attractive play area. They went down a whale sliding board, horsed around on the wooden shrimp boat, and finally, as planned, they made their way up into the plastic tunnels overhead. Grant entered through one end, and Christina the other.

Pretty soon, they realized that an aquarium staffer was between them. He looked funny—as big and tall as he was—all crammed into the tunnel. The backpack jutting up from his back like a fat brown turtle didn't help him move along very fast. As Christina continued to climb on hands and knees from one end, and Grant the other...soon, the boy was trapped between them.

At first, the boy looked aggravated. Then he looked mad. "Get outta my way, you kids. I'm not here to hurt you. But everywhere I go you seem to be in my face. That's the only reason I followed you over here is to tell you to get lost."

"I think everywhere we go, you seem to be there, too," Christina said.

"Well, you kids should have minded your own

business, you know," the boy said angrily. "And if you know what's good for you, you will move out of my way right now!"

"We're going to go and tell on you right now!" said Grant. He began to crawl as fast as he could through the tunnel. The boy chased after him as fast as he could. As they neared the end of the tunnel, Grant scampered out. The boy was close behind, breathing hard. He reached out and almost grabbed Grant by the tail of his shirt. Then the boy looked up and saw a group of frowning adults waiting to capture him.

He twisted and squirmed until he finally got turned around, only to discover that Christina was right behind him blocking his way. "Oh, no you don't!" said Christina. "Your fishy follies are over!"

Angrily, the boy backed out of the tunnel where a security guard helped him to his feet and held him in his grasp. The boy hung his head and let the backpack slide to the floor. The security officer picked up the backpack and led the boy off.

"Where have you been?" asked Mimi. "We've been waiting here for you for much longer than the PLAN."

"I think Grant and Christina have been doing something you don't usually do in an aquarium," said Papa.

"What's that?" asked Mimi.

"Fishing!" said Papa.

"And most importantly," said Christina, "we caught a Big Fish!"

The Big Fish

Later, in the aquarium's boardroom, they all sat around a large table. The boy was slumped in his chair.

"Can you please explain what you were up to and why?" the security guard asked sternly. "Before we call the police."

The boy looked very glum. "Look," he finally said. "I really didn't mean any harm. I just think fish should be free."

The security officer glared at the boy. "Even if you feel that way, you certainly can't think it's right to come onto private property and do bad things."

The boy hung his head. "I never, ever would have hurt the fish," the boy promised. "I guess I just wanted to get some attention. I stole a lab coat so I could move around the aquarium more freely. Then, when I thought these kids might have spotted me, I switched to a staff shirt.   I thought if I could interrupt the monitors I might could put my own message on the screens—about saving the fish—but I never could get it to work."

"And what about the pink coloring in the Beluga tank?" Mimi demanded.

"It was just a prank to have people think something was wrong," the boy said. "I know it was stupid, but it was just harmless food coloring."

"But you pushed Grant into the tank," groused Papa. "He could have drowned!"

The boy looked very upset.   "It was an accident! He thought I pushed him on purpose, but it was just the handle of the scoop. I didn't run off until I saw that he could swim good enough...as good as a fish, in fact!"   Grant beamed.

"And the tainted fish food?" asked the security officer.

"It wasn't tainted at all," the boy swore. "I would never hurt the fish. I didn't tamper with the food...I just altered the test results when no one was looking."

"I guess you had a lot of other schemes up your sleeve?" asked Mimi.

Once more, the boy hung his head. "I guess so," he admitted. "But I had to stop and try to scare these two kids off first. They stayed on me like the golden trevally on the whale sharks. I couldn't shake them off my case," he grumbled.

Mimi sighed. "Well, if there's a SITUATION, they're always on the case."

"And if there's a mystery to solve, they're bound to be right in the middle of it," Papa agreed.

Grant and Christina sat tall and looked proud of themselves.

"But it would have been much better if they had just come and told us their suspicions," Mimi said, pointing a red-painted fingernail at both of her grandchildren.

"Instead of being so stubborn and independent," said Papa with a scowl, but the kids could tell he was proud of them.

Finally, Mr. Marcus, who had been quiet this entire time, spoke up. "Well, as William Shakespeare once said: All's well that ends well. This aquarium is all about education...and I think that the first person who needs to be educated about our mission is this young man." He looked directly at the boy. "If you are a friend of fish, as you say you are, I think you can come to understand that we are actually on the same side of the fish fence."

Everyone looked at the boy. "You know, sir, I apologize for all the trouble I've caused...and I think you're right. The longer I was around the aquarium today, the more I realized what a great job you have done. Just being around the fish and the staff made me want to work here."

"Then you got off to a pretty bad start, kid," said the security officer.

"Yes sir, I know, and I apologize again. I feel pretty stupid, now. I know I'm in big trouble here." He looked very, very worried and very, very scared.

For a moment no one spoke. Then, suddenly, Grant's eyes got very big and bright and he snapped his fingers loudly. "Hey, everyone," he said. "I think I have a PLAN!"

16

Fish Sticks

"Oh, no, not another plan," moaned Christina.

But the PLAN Grant had was really more like a punishment to him. "See," he said. "When I get in trouble at home, I always get put into Time Out."

"He's in Time Out a lot!" Christina volunteered.

"Hush, Christina," Mimi said. "Let your brother finish."

Christina frowned and Grant continued. "And when I'm in Time Out, Mom doesn't let me just sit there...she makes me read books or write reports or sweep or some other chore...soooooooo..."

Before Grant could finish, Christina butted

in. "So, Grant, you mean instead of going to jail this guy could sort of work his way out of trouble doing chores around the aquarium?"

"Yeah," said Grant.

"I would!" the boy cried. "I would work really, really hard. I would repay any damage I've done. I would be the best employee you ever had."

Everyone turned and looked at Mr. Marcus.

"Weren't you ever young and dumb?" Grant asked.

Mimi turned beet red. "Grant!" she said. "HUSH!"

Grant folded his arms across his chest and scowled and skulked down into his seat like his feelings were hurt. "I just meant we all make mistakes, right?"

Christina could see a little twinkle in Mr. Marcus's eye. Finally, he smiled. "Yes," he said, "everyone makes mistakes. But this is a pretty serious one."

"I PROMISE!" said the boy. "I'll do anything you say. I'd love to work with Ralph and Norton, for example."

"I think that's a little high on the food chain, kid," said Papa. "If I were in charge, I'd start you out sweeping the parking lot."

Mimi said, "I have an idea. Let us leave and let Mr. Marcus handle this how he wants to." She stood up, as did Papa, and reluctantly, so did Christina and Grant.

As they headed out of the room, Grant turned around with a worried look on his face and pleaded, "Just don't feed him to the piranha, please?"

Six Months Later...

Six months later, Mimi, Papa, Grant, and Christina returned to the aquarium. Mimi's mystery book was all finished. Papa was going to apply to be a volunteer at the aquarium. Grant had grown two inches taller. Christina was just about ready to celebrate her birthday.

The aquarium was still as popular as ever. People came from all over the world to visit. When they went inside, Christina said, "Why don't we go to the 3-D movie first?"

"Yeah," said Grant, "it's so cool!"

Mimi and Papa nodded and the kids ran up the staircase. Once they had tickets and went inside the theater, a boy in a blue coat with big glasses pretending to be a professor began to tell the crowd about the aquarium and the fish and the movie. He sounded very enthusiastic and excited.

"Hey," said Grant, "isn't that..."

Christina looked hard at the boy and laughed. "Yes," she said. "That's our fishy friend. I think he got a promotion?"

As visitors began to file into the auditorium, the boy came over and shook all their hands. "Hi," he said. "It's great to see you. Listen, I have a PLAN."

Mimi and Papa looked very suspicious. Grant and Christina looked puzzled.

"No, really," the boy said with a big grin. "After the movie, I'm off my shift so why don't we go to the cafeteria and I'll treat you all to cookies and ice cream."

Mimi smiled.

Papa nodded.

Christina grinned.

And Grant said, "Now that's what I call REAL fish food!"

The End

About the Series Creator

Carole Marsh is a native of Marietta, Georgia. She has created and written many mystery books for children over the last 25 years. She always wished that Atlanta had a river running through it..."and now, it sort of does!" she says. Christina and Grant are her real-life grandchildren. They call her Mimi. They often go on adventures with her and their grandfather, Bob Longmeyer, whom they call Papa. Mimi and Papa had an aquarium but it was just filled with colorful paper fish. "We travel too much," says Ms. Marsh. They have visited most of the major aquariums in America, as well as many smaller ones. "Never pass up an aquarium," the author recommends. "Each one is different and you will always learn something new and be surprised at least once!" The author currently lives in Peachtree City, Georgia where she is the Founder and CEO of Gallopade International, a children's book and educational product publishing company. You can contact her at carole@gallopade.com.

BUILT-IN BOOK CLUB
Talk About It!

1. Have you ever been to an aquarium? Which one(s)? What was your visit like?

2. Have you ever thought about all the hard work that goes on behind the scenes in an aquarium? What are some of those jobs? Would you like to have one?

3. How is an aquarium like a zoo? Different from a zoo?

4. Would you like to have grandparents like Mimi and Papa who took you all around the world on adventures to solve mysteries? Do you think Mimi and Papa and Grant and Christina are real or fictional characters, or both?

5. Why did the boy want to cause trouble in the aquarium? How could he have expressed his protest in a better way?

6. What did Grant do when he got pushed in the big fish tank? What would you have done?

7. How does Christina use her "little gray cells" to solve a mystery?

8. In which gallery would you have liked to been along on their adventure the most?

9. If you could be a fish or sea creature, which one would you be? Why?

10. Why was Grant worried that the boy might get fed to the piranha? What kind of fish are they?

11. What is an aquarist?

12. What is icthyology?

13. Did you wonder how Ralph and Norton got their names? Papa knew, but Christina and Grant never found out. Ask some adults or do some research to see if you can find out the answer!

Bring It to Life!

Activities: These are great for pre- or post-aquarium visits, an armchair aquarium visit, birthday parties, or more!

Make a Jell-O® and Gummi Fish Aquarium!

Make 1 large or small individual aquariums. Use plastic fish bowls or any clear container. Make as many packages of blue or green gelatin desert as you need to fill your bowl 2/3 full. You can use ice cubes instead of water to cool the gelatin down and help it chill faster, if you wish. Pour the cooled, but not yet jelled, gelatin mixture into the bowl. Add gummi fish, candy "gravel," leafy greens for seaweed, or any other edible items to your bowl. Chill until completely jelled. Show it off, then eat it!

Create your own "Go Fish" card deck!

On white or colored unlined index cards, have each student (or work in pairs) draw a fish or sea creature on one side of the card. Be sure to put the name of the creature and a number for points, from 1-10. Each card should be duplicated so that there are 2 of every card. After you have completed the "deck," let students play "Go Fish!" by dealing out the cards and matching them until they make pairs, then adding up their points to see who wins.

Fish Finder!

Have students draw a fish or sea creature on an 8.5x11 piece of white construction paper. Have them use resources such as books, encyclopedias, etc. so they can include as much detail and correct coloring as possible. Each student should learn or memorize 3-5 facts about the fish or creature they select. Pin the pictures on the back of each student. Let them walk around or stand up one at the time. Other students get to ask questions such as, "Do you have fins?" until they are able to identify the fish or sea creature. Let the student turn around and show their picture, then share a few facts they have learned.

Scavenger Hunt!

Want to have some fun? Let's go on a scavenger hunt! Go online to www.carolemarshmysteries.com and get a list of *awesome* things to find at an aquarium!

1. Read the book.
2. Visit an aquarium.
3. Go on a scavenger hunt.

Sounds like fun to me!

Pop Quiz!

Hey, Kids! Take this quiz to see what you have learned!

1. What is the largest species of fish on earth?

2. What species of whale is the most endangered?

3. What color is a beluga whale?

4. What kind of "home" do hermit crabs live in—and swap out—from time to time?

5. How do you feed an octopus?

6. Penguins live in what kind of climate?

Tech Connects!

Hey, Kids!
Visit **www.carolemarshmysteries.com** to:

- Join the Carole Marsh Mysteries
  Fan Club!

- Learn the history of aquariums!

- Get a preview of the real-life Georgia
  Aquarium exhibits!

- Download a dot-to-dot fish!

- Download a coloring page!

- Download an aquarium matching activity!

- Download a Pop Quiz!

- Download a Scavenger Hunt!